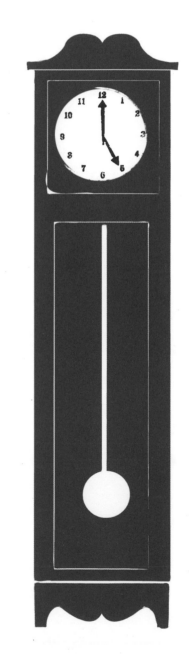

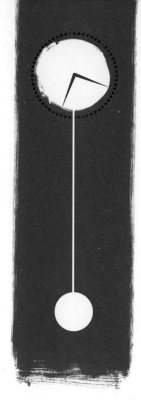

For Mattie and Bill

First U.S. edition 2014
First published in Great Britain in 2012 by Orchard Books, London

Library of Congress Catalog Card Number pending
ISBN 978-0-7636-6826-6

14 15 16 17 18 19 SWT 10 9 8 7 6 5 4 3 2 1

Printed in Dongguan, Guangdong, China

This book was typeset in American Typewriter.
The illustrations were created digitally.

Candlewick Press
99 Dover Street
Somerville, Massachusetts 02144

visit us at www.candlewick.com

Hickory Dickory
DOG

Alison Murray

CANDLEWICK PRESS

Hickory, dickory, dock,
A dog, a boy . . .

a clock!

The day's begun,

It's time for fun!

Hickory, dickory, dock.

Hickory, dickory, dear, Rufus must stay here.

There's a whine and a pine,

And a wet-paint sign. Hickory, dickory, dear.

Hickory, dickory, dare,

NO DOGS ALLOWED

Dogs aren't allowed in there.

A sneaky peek through . . .

Then a **hullabaloo!**

Hickory, dickory, dare.

Hickory, dickory, dee,

Haroo!

Hurrah!

Yippee!

The clock strikes eleven,

It's make-a-mess heaven!

Hickory, dickory, dee.

Hickory, lickery, lunch,
Some yummy food to munch.

The clock strikes noon,

Zack's dropped his spoon!
Hickory, lickery, lunch.

Hickory, dickory, doo,
Uh-oh! A glob of glue!

The weather is fine . . .

So it's garden time.

Hickory, dickory, doo.

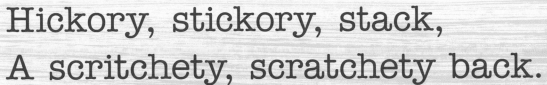

Hickory, stickory, stack,
A scritchety, scratchety back.

Time is up, you mucky pup!
Hickory, stickory, stack.

Higglety, pigglety, pup,
It's home to clean you up!

The clock strikes five.

Slip,

slide,

crash . . .

Hickory, flickory, fly, Rufus still needs to get dry.

First a bit of an itch.

Then a twist and a twitch.

Hickory, flickory, fly.

Hickory, dickory, dock,

A dog, a boy, a clock.

Now it's time
For the end of the rhyme . . .

Hickory, dickory, dog.